I like n
toothpas
strawb
for b

For
Ayeishah

First published in 2015 by Nosy Crow Ltd

The Crow's Nest, 10a Lant Street, London SE1 1QR

www.nosycrow.com

ISBN 978 0 85763 311 8 (HB)

ISBN 978 0 85763 312 5 (PB)

Nosy Crow and associated logos are trademarks and/or registered trademarks of Nosy Crow Ltd.

Text and illustrations copyright © Yasmeen Ismail 2015

The right of Yasmeen Ismail to be identified as the author and illustrator of this work has been asserted.

A CIP catalogue record for this book is available from the British Library.

Printed in China by Imago

Papers used by Nosy Crow are made from wood grown in sustainable forests.

1 3 5 7 9 8 6 4 2 (HB)

1 3 5 7 9 8 6 4 2 (PB)

Greta and Gracie were sisters.

Greta was bigger because she was one year,

six months and three days older than Gracie.

They both had the same smile, the same hoppity-skip walk

and their names both began with G, too. But . . .

When I was your age I was much taller than you are now. I could even reach the kitchen counter on my tippy-toes! It's nice being taller. It makes me look more elegant, don't you think?

Anyway, it must be hard being <u>so</u> short...

. . . Greta was chitty-chatty and Gracie was quiet.
That was just fine because
Greta loved talking to Gracie,
and Gracie loved listening.

Most of the time.

It was Christmas Eve and Greta and Gracie were busy colouring in.

Greta had the red, green, yellow, blue AND black crayons.

Gracie had the brown crayon.

Gracie was still colouring in.
She wanted her picture of Father Christmas
to be just right.

Do you think
Father Christmas
has a bike?

Don't be silly, Gracie.
Father Christmas has a
sleigh, not a bike.
And his boots are BLACK,
not brown.
Anyway, colouring-in is boring.
Let's get our coats and go
outside.

So Greta and Gracie pulled on their jackets and went to help decorate the big tree in the village.

Do you think Father Christmas decorates his Christmas tree?

I don't think so. He has elves to do things like that. Did you know that there are 597 elves in the North Pole? Or maybe it's 598?

Christmas decorations

Whilst Greta was busy thinking about elves,
Gracie looked for the star in the big box of decorations.
She was just getting ready to climb the ladder and put it
on the tree when Greta came over.

You're too **LITTLE** and I've climbed ladders before. I'll pop it on the tree and then we'll go to the shop.

So Greta popped the star on the top of the tree.

The shop was very busy.
Gracie wanted to buy some
red ribbon for wrapping
presents, but it was too noisy.
Everyone from the village
seemed to be there.

Excuse me, Mrs Goose.

Excuse me, Mrs Goose.

I'll do it. You're too QUIET.
And anyway, Father Christmas
only likes gold ribbon.

So Greta asked for the gold ribbon.

Mrs Goose chatted to Gracie as she carefully counted out her coins.

You must be excited about Christmas, Gracie. What do you think Father Christmas is like?

Oh! Father Christmas is just WONDERFUL! He is the best and nicest man and he has a sleigh and reindeer and they give presents to good little girls and boys and he has a HAT and a red coat and a big white bushy beard and he eats BISCUITS! You can write him a letter and he'll come and visit and say "Ho! Ho! Ho!" and he puts things in stockings and he wears BIG BOOTS so his feet are warm and he has BIG buttons on his coat and they are so shiny and sparkly.

He is
magic.

On the way home, Greta said there was just time
to go to the ice-skating rink.

Let's go fast!

Can you twirl as quickly as me?

No Gracie! Like this! Like this!

And now stand on one leg!
Like this!
Like this!
And stretch your arms!
Like this!
Like this!
Like this!

But Gracie decided to go very slowly on the ice.

I don't like going fast, it makes me feel wobbly in my tummy. I might fall over. Do you think Father Christmas likes to skate?

That night, Gracie went to bed. She was listening to Greta snore when she heard a funny noise.

Could that be Father Christmas?

I must not rush. It's good to be SLOW.

Gracie slipped out of bed and opened the bedroom door very carefully so it didn't squeak even the tiniest bit.

She tiptoed along the hallway,
so her feet didn't make a single sound.

The sitting room door was a tiny bit open,
and a little bit of light shone across the hall floor.

Gracie squeezed through the crack.

And there, in the sitting room, was . . .

. . . Father Christmas!

Hello Gracie! What a good thing that you're here. Perhaps you can help me.

It's you!

So Gracie helped Father Christmas with all the parcels
and then they sat together eating biscuits and drinking milk.
They talked about all sorts of things and Gracie asked Father Christmas
all the questions she wanted to, until it was time for him to go on his way.

The next morning, Greta
woke Gracie up very early.

He's been! He's been, Gracie! The biscuits have all been eaten, so he must have liked them. There are loads of presents under the tree. I haven't counted them all yet, but there is a lot. I hope the big ones are for me. We've both got full stockings, too...

Gracie opened her mouth to tell Greta about meeting Father Christmas, but Greta was already pulling her towards the sitting room.

There they found two excitingly knobbly
stockings and a pile of parcels.
Each of the stockings had a label on it.

Look! This one's
for you, Gracie.
I'll read the label.

For Gracie,
Thank you for your help.
It was very nice to meet
you. Love Father
Christmas

You saw Father Christmas?

Yes, I did, and he was sitting right here when I saw him first and he had brown boots and a big red coat and a big sack full of presents that had red ribbon and gold ribbon and blue ribbon and green ribbon.

ALL THE RIBBONS!

And he told me all about his reindeer and what they like to eat and he was really kind and he had a big white beard and twinkly eyes and he asked me to help him.

Come on, Greta,
Let's open our
          presents...

For Greta

. . . and for once, Greta did not say one single word.

Merry Christmas!